# Raven and Rat

EMILY JACOBS

For Summer and Esme.

# MAJIKA

In a parallel universe not that far from earth, floats the magical world of MAJIKA. This mystical land is shaped like a skull. Its shape is no coincidence. A very, VERY important crystal skull sits on a golden pillar in Majika's Royal Palace. It's fan-tabulous! Sparkling purple crystal bling, – with huge diamond teeth. In human world it would be worth more money than the Crown Jewels.

The crystal skull is the beating heart of Majika's magic – THE LAND NEEDS IT TO SURVIVE.

Tales of Majika and the crystal skull have been whispered about from generation to generation. Some children claim to have seen the floating skull island. Adults have laughed at their snotty kid's nonsense tales. But, IT IS possible. When rain drops flutter down and mix with rays of sunshine... at that moment, the moment just before a rainbow appears - if you believe in magic...you will see it too.

There are about 7.8 billion humans in the world. Excitingly a few giant handfuls of them are not just boring old humans. I am going to tell you a secret. You may already know though. You may be one of them! Many years ago, long before you were born, a little bit of Majika's magic escaped. A sorcerer came to earth to learn about us humans but the portal between our worlds had not closed properly. When the sorcerer realised - it was too late. Magic had fallen over earth. It rained down over chosen new-born babies for years to come. The magic blessed them with a special power. Majika call these children – Gifted humans.

Majika's earth walkers and fairies monitor the Gifted humans closely, making sure they don't draw attention to their powers. Or even worse, use them to harm others! Once a young boy deliberately grew as tall as the Eiffel Tower. Humans were terrified, the fairies had to shower him with shrinking dust then convince the gullible humans it was a free magic show.

Very occasionally Majika's wise, old gatekeeper will agree, after much persuasion and a bag of nuts, to allow a Gifted human to visit. But this time the Gifted human coming to Majika was not through choice. It was a matter of destiny.

# DREAMS

Have you ever dreamt a dream so real that you woke up and asked yourself - *was I really dreaming?*

This was the case for ten-year-old Raven Redstone. She was having some crazy weird dreams – all about fairies, candy floss clouds and a freaky blue-eyed bird that shape shifted into a lady. This lady had long silvery hair, wrinkly skin and bright blue eyes that sparkled like glitter. She had been popping up like a bad smell every time Raven fell asleep, shouting about a crystal skull that had been stolen from its golden pillar. Raven was beginning to get quite annoyed with herself and her silly dreams. She blamed her parents for forcing her to move home.

Raven had moved house two weeks ago. Thanks to her workaholic parents she had to spend the summer holidays in a new town, with a new nanny. Even worse, she had to start a new school after the holidays. This was worse than eating a bath tub full of brussel sprouts. Being different, Raven found it hard to make friends. No one ever believed that she could speak to animals. But it was true. Raven was born on a cool crisp evening on the first day in January. On this very evening the fairies danced in joy. Another child had been born with a gift. Raven COULD speak to animals. No ant was too small no giraffe was too tall, she could speak to them all! Her gift was a simple one. She couldn't shoot fireballs from her hands, fly or grow the size of the Eiffel Tower. But little did Raven know that when she was born a prophecy was written. A sorcerer said *the dark-haired beauty that could speak to animals would one day save the magical land of Majika.*

Raven's best friend was her pet rat called Rat. She

5

had rescued Rat from the snarling fangs of a fat cat. She had to trade the cat five tins of tuna for the rat's life. Raven's parents were outraged when she brought the vermin home. But, after a vet told Mr and Mrs Redstone the rat had no deadly diseases, they allowed Raven to keep him. This came with one condition – she was forbidden to talk to animals in public. She was to act 'normal.' Raven wondered how anyone could act normal. After all, was being normal not just being yourself? But she loved the fat cheeky rat so much she agreed.

Night had fallen again. The wind was rattling off Raven's bedroom window. She jumped up and secured the latch. Rat was snoring loudly on his feather pillow dreaming about peanut butter. She switched off her night lamp and closed her eyes hoping for a peaceful sleep with NO interruptions. But unbeknown to Raven, little people with silvery wings and multi coloured dresses were giggling behind her blue curtains. They had the teleportation potion ready. The dream fairies were bursting with excitement. It was time for Raven to go to the land of Majika. The gatekeeper was waiting for her.

# THE GATEKEEPER

It was the damp smell that woke Raven up. It smelt like a wheelbarrow full of cheesy socks. She opened her eyes. Her mouth went dry. Her throat tightened.

"Greetings Raven Redstone," said a squirrel with a loud posh voice. He held a stethoscope on her chest. He listened and nodded looking pleased with what he heard. The peculiar red squirrel was very smart in a blue and white stripy waistcoat and a matching bow tie.  He pushed up his thick round glasses and began puffing on a pipe. Puffs of smoke danced upwards, shaped like musical notes.

"Ouch," Raven pinched herself on the arm. She was not dreaming. She rubbed her arm and sat up.

She was in a small, damp shed surrounded by

baskets full of nuts.  A big red velvet chair looked out of place in the corner. And looking out the small poky window she could see large fluffy pink clouds.

"Personality suitable for Majika," the squirrel held out a paw after his examination. Raven offered her thumb to shake.

"Rovi's the name – handsome I know," Rovi bowed. Raven noticed her black backpack beside her. It started to move.

"My oh my, this is not ideal!" Rovi was surprised as Rat stumbled out the bag half asleep. Rat's eyes opened. He looked around and then screamed.

"Where in the diddly, dreadful, damp dungeons are we?" Rat asked.

"I'm not sure, Rat."

"Raven Redstone and mouse – "

"RAT!" Raven and Rat shout at the same time. Rat took great offence being referred to as a mouse.

"Where are my manners. Please to meet you Miss Raven Redstone and RAT. I am Rovi, gatekeeper of

Majika."

Raven and Rat look at each other and start to laugh. They laugh and laugh until they realise Rovi is not laughing. In fact, he looks super-duper serious.

Rovi tells Raven that the lady she was dreaming about was very real and her name is Esmerelda. Esmerelda is an Earth Walker – human on earth but a mystical bird in Majika. Esmerelda had been on a mission to let Raven know that Majika needed her help.

"You are the gatekeeper?" Raven tried not to laugh again.

"What did you expect? A slobbering troll, or a monster monkey?!"

Before Raven could spit out a million questions, faint screams came from outside. Rovi pulled a telescope from out of mid-air and flung open a window. The air smelt sweet.

"It's happening!" he screamed. Rovi began frantically raiding through a cupboard. CLASH,

BANG, THUMP…he threw several strange objects over his shoulders before finding what he was looking for.

Raven looked through the telescope curiously. What she saw was terrible, like a bad nightmare. Far in the distance, heading in their direction, was an evil grey mist. It was turning everything and everyone to stone. A field of football sized strawberries - now stone. A lady making a huge pot of jam - now stone. Every ant, bunny, tree and flower…still as stone.

"I want to go home," cried Rat. Even the sweet smell of strawberries couldn't stop him trembling.

Rovi handed Raven a dusty old scroll tied up with stained string.

"This is your map to get you to the Royal Palace. You must be there by sunset on your second day. It is life or death Raven. Be there by the second day, follow the map."

"SECOND DAY!" Rat was most displeased.

"Your go home potion," said Rovi handing Raven a

test tube with a bubbling yellow liquid secured with a brown cork.

"Drink this and you will find yourself back home."

"Phew I'll have my drop now," begged Rat.

"You MUST find the stolen crystal skull and return it to the Royal Palace. This is the only thing that will stop the evil mist." Rovi chanted some words and a door appeared in the shed.

"Why me?" asked Raven.

"Because of the prophecy, it is your destiny to save Majika!" The shed started to shake, like an aeroplane experiencing turbulence. A cool wind started to wisp around them. It was getting faster and noisier. Whooshing in and out of every corner.

"But how will I find the skull?" Raven asked the wind now pushing her towards the door.

"Follow the map Raven. You will find a way! Good luck Raven and mouse." Rovi said with a cheeky smile before vanishing into thin air.

Raven was lost for words. This had to be the weirdest, craziest most exciting thing that had ever happened to her. If she drunk the yellow potion she would be back home, sleeping or bored. She was craving an adventure. It was as inviting as ripping open Christmas presents.

"For the love of peanut butter." Rat sighed, seeing the sparkle of adventure twinkle in Raven's eyes.

"Don't worry Rat, I'll take care of you," she said zipping him safely in and securing the bag on her back. Raven closed her eyes and stepped forward into thin air. She began to fall, tumbling through pink candy floss clouds. She yelled loudly seeing an oversized purple toadstool shooting up towards her.

# ALFIE

The toadstool offered a soft landing. Raven slid off the huge bouncy toadstool and fell with a thud on mushy ground. Mud splattered up her yellow wellies. She opened her bag. Rat was shaking with his eyes closed, clutching the go home potion.

"Are you OK?"

"OK would be a thunderstorm, or your mum buying me chocolate spread instead of peanut butter, or the time your cousin tried to flush me down the toilet. But this Raven – IS NOT OK!" screamed Rat, whiskers twitching.

A cold gust of air whooshed past Raven. She froze looking at the animal shaped head stones dotted around. She was in an animal cemetery. She patted Rat on the head and zipped up the bag. The cold air was not just wind. It was a ghost, in the

14

shape of a bear! More ghosts appeared hovering all around. A little hamster was playing tag with a giant bear, while a cat slept with a smile. They all looked so happy floating around playfully.

Raven untied the scroll to study the map as a dragon ghost flew past with an almighty SWOOSH! She carefully studied the directions to the Royal Palace.

*Follow the pink pebble path to the Cave of Doom.*

She closed a metal gate to the cemetery. The gate had a silver sign that read -

"Brave Earth Walkers. Humans on earth and animals in Majika." In front of her now was the pink pebble path woven through the field and up into the hills. It leads to the Cave of Doom - a dot far in the distance.

The grey sky was clearing, sun beams gleamed through the pink clouds. *Pink clouds.* The same candy floss clouds Raven had dreamt about.

Rat was protesting he needed air. Raven let him out.

"Well, this is delightful….. NOT!" he screamed again.

"Sshhh Rat," she heard someone crying. It was coming from the clouds.

The next thing a boy fell from the sky, and landed with a thud in front of them. Mud splashed up on his face.

"It's raining boys?" Rat looked up in case any more little people were going to squash him.

*He ate his way through a candy floss cloud*…Raven remembered her dream as the boy stood up dusting bits of pink fluff from his brown dungarees. His face was a mass of freckles and mud. But it was the ears which made Rat curious. They pointed upwards through his light brown hair. Shaped like skinny triangles.

"Hello," greeted the boy through tears and snot. He pulled a tissue from his pocket and blew loudly. Then used another tissue to wipe away the mud.

"Are you ok?"

"Do I look ok?" cried the boy.

"Eh no," said Rat.

Raven gave Rat a look.

"Hi I'm Raven," she held out her hand.

"Alfie's the name. No family, no home…" he began to cry again.

"What happened?" Raven felt sorry for Alfie crying like a baby. He cried very loudly, the ghosts from the cemetery vanished.

"Elphinstone Valley, my family…everything has been turned to stone!" Alfie sobbed. He told them how he had snuck away to eat candy floss clouds and watched in horror as the evil mist approached. He ran and ran until he could run no more.

"You're an elf?" Raven asked.

"Of course, what else would I be?" Alfie wiped his eyes, a light bulb sparked in his head.

  Before Raven could answer the elf jumped and clicked his heels together. He began to talk at record speed. He was talking so fast and swirling in circles.

Raven and Rat looked at each other.

"I preferred his tears," yawned Rat.

"You're the dark-haired girl from the prophecy?" Alfie said calming down.

"I guess..." Raven shrugged.

"So, what's the plan?" asked Alfie. He knew all about the stolen Crystal Skull and the prophecy of the black- haired girl that can speak to animals. It was a key topic at Elphinstone Academy.

"My mission is to get to the palace and return the crystal skull, no idea how but Rovi said it will unfold with time," Raven explained to Alfie handing him the scroll.

"Oh snotbags," cried Alfie his long thin finger pointing at the Cave of Doom.

"Bad?" asked Raven with a gulp.

"Death!" Alfie exclaimed!

"But Rovi said I MUST stick to this exact map."

"Oh, grizzling Grumpkins. Cave of Doom it is. If we are alive tomorrow, I'll swim down Lemonpop River in my underpants."

Raven gulped again. That was something she did

NOT want to see. But she did hope to be alive.

# SILVERDRAKE

The dragon's eyes were burning red. His shining yellow teeth stood tall as an elephant's trunk! His gigantic body was covered in a suit of armor – midnight blue tough scales. As its large mouth opened, dark smoke puffed out its bulging nostrils. He knew the human girl was coming. He could smell her!

As Raven approached the Cave of Doom, she wondered what the noise was. Alfie had warned her about the deadly dragon. His teeth were clattering together. He was nervous. Raven reminded herself that they must, must, MUST pass through the cave. It was the quickest way to Grumpkin Forrest.

"Wait here," she whispered to Alfie and Rat.

"You don't have to tell me twice," muttered Alfie jumping back a step.

"Hello!" shouted Raven trying to sound as brave as a bear. The sunlight flooding in the cave shone upon bundles of bones. There were big bones, small bones, fat bones, skinny bones. So many bones all piled high like an evil tower! She was starting to think this maybe wasn't such a good idea. She desperately wanted to get to the palace but she really REALLY did not want to become a BBQ meal for a hungry dragon.

The ground started to tremble and Raven heard an almighty bang as the dragon took a step forward into the warm sunlight. No turning back now.

"He-llo Mr Drag....on," Raven said trying to sound assertive. Frozen with fear, she was close to the most dangerous animal she had ever met in her whole life! The dragon lowered his head down to take a sniff.

"Funny little human," said the dragon.

"Funny big dragon," replied Raven. She slapped her

hand over her mouth. WHOOOPS!!! It was not wise to insult a dragon.

The dragon snorted in shock. Green slime shot past Raven's head.

"That is super gross Mr Dragon. Yuck," she looked at the big pile of gooey snot.

"You can speak to dragons?" his voice was surprised.

"I can speak to animals," replied Raven with a smile. Her fear was beginning to melt away as she heard a kindness in the dragon's voice.

"Silverdrake is my name. Oh, and I can smell the elf and mouse too."

"He's a rat."

"Rat – big mouse, same thing," snorted Silverdrake.

"Do you want to eat us?" Raven asked.

Silverdrake started to laugh. He laughed so loud and hard that he burped a huge ball of grey smoke.

"Pardon me," he apologised for the super loud burp.

"I've already ate," he winked. His red eyes

twinkling.

"Who did you eat?" asked Raven glancing at the piles of bones.

"Can you keep a secret?" asked Silverdrake in a low growling whisper.

"Yes, I can," Raven moved closer tilting her ear.

"The bones were here long before me. The moon is my source of energy. My scales bath in the moonlight that gleam in the cave at night."

"Why don't you fly across the valley at night?" Raven remembered Alfie saying the dragon never, ever leaves the cave.

"Ah…that's another story for another day," Silverdrake said before changing the subject to Raven's mission.

Raven waved to Alfie and Rat that it was safe. They were not going to be dragon food.

Alfie ran past Silverdrake screaming at the top of his voice. He was terrified and paying no attention to where he was going. He ran straight into a tower of bones. CLASH, BANG, TUMBLE!

As Raven laughed at Alfie's clumsiness, she noticed sadness in Silverdrake's eyes. He dropped his head.

"Oh, please don't be offended by Alfie," said Raven. "He is a big wimp!"

"I'm used to it. But it is nice to hear laughter."

"You must fly somewhere safer?" Raven placed a hand on Silverdrake's face. She liked the dragon. She told him about her mission, the scroll and the deadly mist heading his way. His scales were surprisingly smooth but very cold. She knew it wouldn't be long until the grey stone mist reached the caves. Even a flame breathing, strong dragon was no force to stop it. The dark magic could only be stopped by returning the crystal skull to its rightful place in the palace. And Rovi said if Raven follows this map, she will find the way.

"Go now little warrior, you must hurry."

"What about you?" Raven asked.

"How funny. A small human girl worried about a big scary dragon." Silverdrake looked like he was smiling.

"You might look a bit scary, but you are kind and gentle," Raven placed her hand on his cool scale. She was furious with Alfie and Rat judging the dragon by his appearance. Her mum always told her never to judge a book by its cover and now she knew why.

Silverdrake poked his head out the cave.

"GO NOW little Raven - be safe!" he could see it. The grey stone mist was getting closer - leaving a trail of destruction in its path. It showed no mercy.

# GRUMPKIN FORREST

Raven was grateful for the glow worms paving the way through the dark tunnel. It had been a long, damp walk and Alfie's singing was torture. He really was the worst singer she had ever heard.

It was getting late, everyone was tired, hungry and cold. Raven thought of her new home – her big comfy bed, the fridge full of food, a warm shower.

"Grumpkins better have some grumpkin goodness," moaned Alfie, slumping down onto a soft patch of grass. He pulled a white handkerchief from his deep pocket and wiped his sweaty brow. "It is exhausting battling dragons and trekking through dark dangerous tunnels."

Raven ignored Alfie's exaggerations and glanced around. Night had fallen - a billion bright white stars twinkled far in the distance. A half-moon was lighting up the forest like a neon playground. It was very beautiful. Flowers shone white, yellow, pink and blue like glow sticks around the tree trunks. Raven had to tilt her head flat back to follow the trees to the sky.

"Erm…Alfie." Alfie had fallen asleep on the damp mossy grass. He was snoring and drooling all over the place.

"Great," said Raven, nudging her new snoring friend. What a pair of helpers; Rat sleeping in her backpack and Alfie sleeping in the middle of a forest. Raven pulled out her map and looked around for some clues. She had no idea where to find a Grumpkin or what they even looked like.

"Hello," she shouted softly. A spark of light came from the tree. It moved so fast.

"You're the girl from the prophecy? Small, silly human girl!" laughed a blonde fairy tugging at Ravens long dark hair.

"Humans have a funny smell, do they not," she

jibbed swooshing her silvery dress.

"I thought fairies were supposed to be nice," Raven said, shocked by the rudeness of something so small.

"What's your name?" Raven asked, trying to make conversation.

"Follow me," snubbed the fairy.

Raven turned to look at Alfie still snoring. He looked so uncomfortable.

"Lazy butt faced ELVES!" the fairy screamed, her pale cheeks turning red with temper.

She flew over to Alfie sprinkling gold dust over his legs. She looked very amused with herself. Alfie was now floating behind them upside down – still sleeping!

"Follow me -" the fairy was off.

Raven had to jog to keep up. She tried to avoid standing on the neon flowers; they were too pretty to be squashed. She could hear chatter and smell smoke. A lot of voices all talking at once, it got louder and louder.

"Put him down, Willow!" shouted a miniature troll jumping out from behind a tree. The odd creature was the height of a toddler with sticky out ears, blue leathery skin and eyes as wide as an egg.

"With pleasure," Willow clicked her tiny fingers and Alfie fell with a thud.

"Ouch," he rubbed his head and wiped some drool from his cheek.

"Mr Grumps!" cried Alfie delighted. He ran over and dropped to his knees his arms wide open.

"My my Alfie. It's been almost three hundred and sixty-five moons." said Mr Grumps slapping Alfie on the back.

"Family well?"

"Still as stone," Alfie looked like he was about to burst into tears again.

"Just this morning my mum was ordering me to apply for my warrior's badge. I snuck away to eat candy floss." Alfie looked ashamed.

"All in good time Alfie." Mr Grumps reassured.

"We have been waiting for you," he said turning his

attention to Raven. Mr Grumps had a mouth full of teeth. He clearly didn't brush for two minutes twice a day. Raven hated brushing her teeth. Her mum nagged her constantly. After meeting Mr Grumps, she will never complain about brushing her teeth again.

"Come, come. All the Grumpkins are sitting around the bonfire, waiting for the ceremony. We have cherry pie and the finest berry juice," he patted his round belly proudly.

What ceremony?" Alfie asked thinking that sounded like something that will take a long time. He just wanted to eat pie.

"Miss Raven is getting presented with the ancient wishing opal," Mr Grumps bowed at Raven like royalty.

"Ahhh so she can make one wish at the royal wishing well!" said Alfie still thinking about pie.

"To return the crystal skull," whispered Raven happy she knew what she had to do.

"We can't stay up very late though. I am told

earthlings need their beauty sleep. Not that that applies to you Miss Raven."

Raven blushed. Willow kicked the air and flew away with steam spouting from her ears.

# RESPONSIBILITY

Raven snuggled into a cosy yellow blanket. She was sleeping in the tallest tree in Grumpkin forest. The branches were huge and squashed together lined with a soft moss. She gazed up at the gigantic stars. They looked like the size of a football. Alfie was sprawled out like a starfish, snoring like a pig. Rats belly was full and he was snuggled up behind Alfie's legs. He had only just got over the trauma of sleeping at an incredible height.

Raven's mind was on the ceremony and Silverdrake. Mr Grumps told her the story of Silverdrake's curse. A dark magic spell had been cast to keep the dragon prisoner in the cave of doom... forever! Nothing could undo his horrible fate. Raven felt so sad for him. She had forced a smile on her face when the grumpkins and fairies gathered in excitement to meet the gifted human that was destined to save their world. Gulp! What a big responsibility. The fuss and drama made Raven realise she did not want to be famous. She had never shaken so many hands or engraved her initials in so many tree trunks. It was all very embarrassing. It was nice to be in the tree. It was peaceful and quiet (except from Alfie's snoring). She pulled her diary and pen from her bag.

*Dear Diary,*

*It's been the craziest, most exciting, scariest day of my life! I've met a new friend. Alfie's weird and funny. I do like him actually, he's not a boy, he is an elf. I think Rat secretly likes him too. Probably because he makes Rat look brave.*

*Everyone is being so nice to me, well...except a little fairy with the temper of a bear. They think I am some sort of hero as I am supposed to save their world. It's really quite embarrassing. The evil mist is travelling across the land and the only way to stop it is to return the crystal skull to the palace. I've got this ancient opal stone now. It's pretty awesome; a million colours swirl through it. Looks cool. And it will grant me one wish at the palaces magic wishing well. I wonder what the skull looks like? Sounds a bit creepy if you ask me. I feel sooo much pressure. I never knew my gift of speaking to animals would come with so much responsibility. I'm lucky though, I have the yellow potion I can drink to go home. I really hope I don't have to drink it before saving Majika.*

*PS: I would give anything for a waffle and chocolate spread right now. The cherry pie was revolting. Not that I would tell Mr Grumps that. I ate it all without being sick and said it tasted fantastic. Lie.*

Raven held tight as Alfie tried to snatch her diary.

"Don't you know it's rude to read a girls diary?" she snapped rubbing her eyes.

"I do like him actually..." said Alfie laughing.

"You're the worst elf I've ever met," shouted Raven annoyed.

"I'm the only elf you have met," chuckled Alfie.

Rat was frozen with fear. He remembered he had to climb back down the ladders in the tree trunk.

He opted to climb in Raven's backpack and imagine he was swimming in a pool of peanut butter instead.

A crowd had gathered around the large tree trunk. The grumpkins and fairies panicked faces looked pleased to see Raven.

"News has come that the mist is now at the Caves of Doom," Mr Grumps said sadly.

Silverdrake. Poor Silverdrake. Raven thought of the cursed dragon now a statue of stone.

"Best be on your way," said Mr Grumps shaking Raven's hand firmly.

Even the sky was sad. Heavy grey clouds looked like they were about to burst.

"Willow will guide you to Lemon Pop River, it's not far."

Willow flew around Raven's head like a torpedo. Surely any fairy but Willow thought Raven. The fairy clearly did not like her. Why? She had no idea.

After saying goodbyes and saying thank you for the ancient opal, disgusting pie and bed for the evening they were off. The evil grey mist wasn't far behind them.

# LEMONPOP RIVER

Raven was struggling to keep up with Willow darting in and out trees, over mossy rocks and little water pools. Alfie and Rat had run ahead. She could hear water. They must almost be at Lemonpop River. Raven was grateful for the woolly pink and purple star jumper the grumpkins knitted for her. It was rather chilly. Raven heard Willow scream. For a little fairy she had a big voice.

Raven ran fast. She hoped it was not the flesh-eating goblins Mr Grumps had warned them about.

What she saw was much worse than flesh eating goblins. It was Alfie...he was standing with nothing but his green underpants!

"A bet is a bet!" shouted Alfie diving into the water.

"Super gross. You only made the bet with yourself!" Raven pulled a face and turned away.

"YUCK, he is disgustingly!" screamed Willow.

Finally, something they could agree on.

Alfie's head was bobbing up and down in the river. His hair now wet and stuck to the side of his cheeks. His ears pointed upwards like weapons.

"Hurry up. Waters fresh," he shouted.

Rat was now standing staring at Alfie, the water current was getting stronger in the breeze.

"Do you think he is insane?" Rat asked.

"Stupid. Stupid. Stupid elf!" Willow flew over to a wooden boat tied up against the grassy bank.

Raven started to laugh as a silver fish tail slapped Alfie on his face. Then she remembered the gatekeeper's instruction 'to be at the palace before sunset of the second day'.

"Times against us naked elf! Get your clothes before we have nightmares." Raven pointed her finger at his bundle of clothes.

Before long they were off - paddling with small

wooden oars. The wind was blowing in their favour, helping the boat glide easily down the river. Along the way Raven saw some of the most beautiful flowers, trees and odd-looking animals. Six-legged deer's and purple bunny rabbits with long fluffy ears that glowed like light bulbs. Butterflies danced around the boat. They looked like they had jumped right out of a cartoon. Vibrant colours all bursting with life. She wondered if they knew what evil was approaching.

Raven could see a big waterhole in the distance where the river ended. They were to get off there and head west through the forest. Raven pulled out her map to double check.

 "Get off here, get off here," Willow appeared like a burst of sparkles from out of nowhere. She had a habit of doing that.

"Thought you'd be long gone," Raven answered tired of Willows bad attitude.

"GET OFF HERE!" her small mouthed screamed in Raven's ear. Fairy spit flew in her eardrum. So gross.

"Goblins," she whispered.

Raven had to slap a hand over Alfie's mouth. He was about to scream.

"Don't be sick on me or I'll pee on your head." Rat jumped on Raven's lap. Alfie had turned a sickly shade of green.

"Evil goblins. Oh, I knew I shouldn't have gone to the strawberry field. I'd rather be Alfie the statue than ripped to shreds by…"

"SHUT UP!" Willow snapped her fingers shooting white sparkling light in Alfie's direction.

"Impressive," nodded Raven as Alfie mumbled unable to speak.

"Won't last long, unfortunately."

They rowed the boat to the grassy bank and quietly (thanks to Willows magic) headed nervously towards the forest.

The trees made spidery shadows on the forest bed. Willow led the way scouring below with a bird's eye view. Then she saw it lurking behind the tree…It pounced out. A small green goblin with creepy burning red eyes stood, smiling. His sharp teeth were pointy like its hideous nose. His nails were ridiculously long. They gleamed like sharpened swords ready for battle.

"Dinner," it chuckled throwing his head back and licking his lips. The goblin pulled a horn from a satchel on his side. Alfie screamed a high pitch scream that would make babies jealous. Then he was sick. Rat scurried to Raven's ankle to avoid Alfie's belching.

"RUN!" screamed Willow charging towards the goblin.

She sprinkled enough dust to tip him upside down. Floating furiously in mid-air he blew the horn. Grungy green drool sprayed everywhere.

"I'll be snacking on you soon human girl," he bellowed after the loud horn had finished echoing through the land. The goblin army had been alerted.

# GOBLINS

Raven and Alfie fell to the ground exhausted. The ground below trembled. The goblin army was not far behind them.

"Please can we go home," Rat sobbed panting like a dog.

He knew by the wild look in Raven's eyes that they were not going home. Not yet.

Raven was angry. Did they not know the prophecy? If they killed her, they would become stone statues – forever.

The palace was a white dot in the distance. All that was between them and the safety of the protective white palace walls was a bare field. The grass was soft and bouncy; springy like a trampoline. Candyfloss clouds hovered all over the place.  Alfie looked at the clouds. It was his greed that had got him muddled up in this adventure. And now his home was stone. They had to return the crystal skull and bring back the magical balance to stop the evil mist.

"You must keep moving," Willow shouted before disappearing into a puff of silver sparkles.

They walked briskly getting their breathing back to normal. Then they heard a rumble from the woods. Raven turned around to see more goblins than she could count. They charged onto the field with one thing on their mind - eating her.

Raven, Rat and Alfie ran fast - their hearts pounding in fear. The goblins ugly wiry bodies bounced and leaped forward hissing like vampires. In a spilt moment of time everything crossed Raven's mind – her mum, dad, the yellow potion, the evil grey mist, the crystal skull and Silverdrake. She felt a stabbing pain in her ankle when a metal claw sunk deep into her skin throwing her to the ground. She howled in pain kicking furiously to break free. Alfie did his best with a stick. He smacked the goblins on the head in an attempt to protect Raven. Rat pounced out, terrified. He cuddled into Raven holding her ankle gushing of blood. They were surrounded.

"Go home Raven and Rat," said Alfie, bravely wondering which goblin was going to kill him. A tear of terror trickled down his cheek.

The goblins started to argue about who would eat which parts. The main debate was over Raven's seemingly tasty heart. Outnumbered and out powered the terrified trio were doomed. Rat held the yellow potion pleading with Raven. Before Raven could answer a shadow cast over them. A blast of blue energy flung the hissing goblins through the air. They landed with a crash in the distance. What flew down from the sky was the most beautiful creature Raven had ever seen.

Alfie was on his knees with his head bowed.

A unicorn landed beside them. Her magical horn

blasted lightning bolts at the goblins. They scurried away like a pack of wild dogs.

Raven was dazzled by the unicorn's beauty. Her coat was as white as snow, her wings glimmered like a midnight moon sparkling on a lake. Wide kind brown eyes met Raven's.

"Greetings gifted one. A pleasure it is, to meet you," she spoke lightly. Her voice danced like music.

"Thank you for saving us," Raven said. Rat nodded too.

"Thank you. Your majesty," shuffled Alfie nervously getting to his feet. He had never met a royal before. He had heard tales of their beauty, and stories of their passion and bravery.

Raven looked at the unicorn. She had not expected the Queen to be a unicorn!

"Lady Majik, from the royal line of magical unicorns," she lowered her head in an official greeting.

"Queen of Majika and protector of the crystal

skull," she continued lowering her knees to the grass.

"Climb on. Time is running out." Lady Majik said urgently.

Alfie was shaking with excitement. The Queen of Majika, his mom would be so proud. Rat was shaking with fear. Raven was trying to stop the bleeding on her ankle.

"Ghastly goblins," said Lady Majik looking at Raven's bleeding wound. Her horn beamed brightly. White sparks danced over to Raven's ankles. Within minutes the trickling blood was sucked back towards the open wound. The wound closed. The skin healed. It was as if it had never happened.

"Magic!" she winked.

"Can't you just use magic to find the Crystal Skull?" snapped Rat. If they were at home this wouldn't have happened in the first place.

Raven repeated the question Rat had just asked. It was a good question.

"The Crystal Skull is the source of our royal magic. It is a pure crystal. It brings the balance of magic into our world - and our world will be no more if it's not returned. Let's go," she ordered.

# ONE WISH

Lady Majik landed gracefully on the cobbled courtyard. It was indeed fit for Royalty. Pots of colourful flowers stood proudly around a magnificent water fountain. Water whished all around a dragon statue. Standing very still and quiet around the perimeter of the walls were tall smartly dressed Elves.

"Elf warriors!" Alfie whispered excitedly waving to one of the elves like his hand was about to fly off. He was ignored.

A row of posh stables with golden railings stood side by side. The name plaques on each stable were encrusted with shiny diamonds. Raven read *Lady Majik, Sunbeam, Lucy, Bramble* before the Queen interrupted her thoughts.

*"A wish from the heart, honest, true let it start. The*

*ancient royals will listen, their powers will glisten. The opal we share with kindness and care. One wish shall be granted, true and rare."* Lady Majik pointed her horn. A large bubble wrapped around Raven scooping her from her feet.

"Hey!" Raven pushed against the bubble. It would not pop. The bubble lifted her in the air. Light as a feather she floated upwards.

"Where is she going?!" Alfie and Rat asked. They watched their friend trapped in a bubble, floating up past the white palace turrets. They felt helpless.

"Calm little ones. She is going to the wishing well." Lady Majik spoke softly.

"High in the sky!!!" Rat was displeased. Even the royals were crazy.

The queen used her horn to make another bubble. It mirrored Raven's. A bubble TV thought Alfie. Raven was sitting crossed legged drifting through candy floss clouds. A small floating island was bobbing about in the sky. The bubble moved towards it like a magnet only stopping when it reached the wishing well.  Raven pushed against the bubble and fell out - flat on her face. Alfie laughed, thinking this was good TV.

Raven stood silently holding the ancient opal tightly.  Her hands felt warm. She slumped on the ground, leaning against the stone wishing well.

"What is she waiting for?" asked another unicorn stepping forward. Alfie presumed it was Sunbeam as she came from her stable.

"Not sure," Lady Majik said sounding a little worried. She had no idea why Raven would pause to make the wish. An evil mist would destroy their land by sunset tomorrow. They needed the crystal skull. Rovi had assured the royals that Raven was not selfish or greedy. She would not use the wish for personal gain.

Raven continued to rub the opal in her hands. She rested her elbows on her knees and dropped her head down. She was deep in thought. Then she jumped to her feet and smiled. Unaware everyone was watching her. Everyone within the palace walls was watching Raven - their hero.

Raven closed her eyes; her head was telling her to wish for the crystal skull, her heart was telling her something else. She looked at the ancient opal now sparkling in her hand. The wishing well was waiting.

Raven took a big breath and spoke loud and clear. "I wish… I wish to break Silverdrake the dragon's curse. I wish him to be free once again," she dropped the ancient opal. It was several seconds before she heard a splash. It echoed loudly. A burst of violet light shot out of the wishing well. It travelled at lightning speed high into the sky before exploding with a bang. A purple firework showered over the whole of Majika.

Silverdrake was free.

"We are doomed," stuttered Alfie. His jaw hanging down.

Rat slapped his paw off his furry forehead. What has Raven done?

# DETECTIVE

The unicorns stared at each other silently as Raven's bubble returned to the courtyard.

Yikes. Raven gulped, so many faces staring at her with disgust.

"Come child," Lady Majik and five other unicorns walked towards the palace. Raven, Alfie and Rat followed quietly behind.

The grand white doors. Inside was a large room with a white marble floor, star shaped windows and stairs that lead to the turrets. In the center of the room was a golden pillar. This was where the crystal skull should be sitting.

Once inside, the doors slammed shut.

Lady Majik and the unicorns lined up by the pillar.

"Please explain?" Lady Majik asked. Her warm friendly voice fading.

"I just couldn't get Silverdrake out my mind," Raven said. This was true, ever since Mr Grumps spoke of his curse; Silverdrake had been popping into her mind all the time.

"Majika… *was* a better place with him," Sunbeam said to her mother. Fire breathing Silverdrake kept the goblins away. The evil creatures had been terrorising the land ever since his curse. Grumpkin forest had lost many good fairies and Grumpkins in battles.

"But there will be no Majika without the Crystal Skull, and his curse may be broken but he may still be a stone statue," reminded Lady Majik.

"Do you keep note of the gifted humans that enter Majika?" Raven asked. An idea was bubbling in her head. She felt like a detective on a mission.

"Yes, Rovi keeps an entry log," Lady Majik said. Her horn beamed then a square hologram appeared in mid-air.

"Greetings your majesty," Rovi tried to spit out some nuts. His cheeks were bulging.

"Rovi I need to see the entry log please." Raven said urgently.

Rovi disappeared and came back with a large brown book.

"What is one doomed squirrel looking for?"

"I need you to check. Did any human have the gift of teleporting?" Raven asked.

The royals looked at each other with puzzled looks.

"I don't suppose you have any peanut butter?" Rat asked his belly rumbling.

Raven glared at him. Alfie, he was also thinking about eating. He longed for more cherry pie.

Rovi flicked through the pages. His nose twitching and bushy tail swaying.

"Ahhh ha! Yes, how could I forget," he shook his cheeks annoyed.

"Darcy, lovely girl that could teleport. Many moons have passed since she was last here though. She would be almost sixteen in human years. Why?"

When Raven was born her dad bought her mum a large ring. It has a huge amethyst stone surrounded by diamonds. Raven remembered a time when her dad lost his job. They became very poor, very quickly. Her mum suggested selling the ring almost every day as it was worth so much money. Raven kept thinking that if that ring was valuable just how much would the crystal skull be worth? She guessed a lot.

"Think about it. Why would anyone steal the skull in Majika? They would destroy their world and themselves. In my world the skull would be worth so much money. And humans seem to love money." Raven said. It was the only thing that made sense.

Before Raven could continue with her plan a burst of sparkles came into the room. It was Willow. Something was very wrong – she was happy!

"Mwahhh, mwahhh, mwah," the fairy done flips of joy over to Raven and kissed her on the cheek three times!

"Are you ill?" Raven asked slowly in complete shock.

"You freed my friend," Willow gushed

For a thousand moons Willow had been begging the Grumpkins to free Silverdrake but they always said NO. They were saving the ancient opal for the prophecy child that could speak to animals!

"Humans aren't all bad after all. I thought Darcy was the only one that wanted to help-" bowed little Willow, she had forgotten her manners in front of royalty.

Lady Majik snorted loudly. Her nostrils flared.

"I'M RIGHT!" shouted Raven.

"What have I missed?" asked Willow confused.

Raven explained. Willow was so annoyed. She did not get tricked. She was the tricker! Darcy told Willow she had come back to Majika to help free Silverdrake. But when her attempts to steal the Grumpkins magical rhyme for the ancient opal stone failed, she said she was going home.

"Disgraceful Darcy!" Willow screamed back to her angry little self.

# MAGIC MAP

Raven pulled out the scroll and unrolled it.

She placed her finger on the map. An arrow was pointing at a mountain behind the palace. It read 'FINAL POINT'.

Everyone stared at Raven and the map. All their eyes could see was her finger pointing at a blank stained piece of paper.

"My oh my, what a sneaky sorcerer. This scroll was made with magic for your eyes only," Rovi sounded hopeful again. Rovi had a theory. Gifted humans could only return home by drinking the gatekeeper's yellow potion. It was the magical law. But the magical law would cease to exist when the grey mist reached the final point in Majika. "It is at this time Darcy will be able to teleport to my world with the Crystal Skull!" Raven said excitedly. She liked the sound of 'Detective Raven'.

The mist was moving faster. The Grumpkin forest, Lemonpop River, Elfinstone Valley was now deadly still. No ant or butterfly, fairy or elf was able to defeat it. Majika would soon be one big stone land. The next stop would be the palace.

"Sunbeam will take you," Lady Majik looked towards her daughter with a trace of sadness. She knew the dangers that she could face. Sunbeam was pacing from side to side, despite being the plumpest she was the fastest unicorn in the whole of the palace.

"Darcy is getting it when we find her," Rat squeaked showing his two front teeth. Rat was very grumpy; he longed for a paw full of peanut butter.

"Maybe you should stay here Rat," suggested Sunbeam.

"Nice try Princess! But where the yellow go home potion goes...I follow!" Rat said in his very serious voice.

After fueling up on bread, cheese and berry juice they were ready. Raven and Alfie were grateful for the navy-blue waterproof jacket and trousers. The rain was battering down the size of golf balls.

"Ride fast, Sunbeam. My magic's weakening. It will hold the mist off for only a short time," Lady Majik opened the gates of the white wall surrounding the palace. Sunbeam nuzzled into her mother's wet damp mane.

"I'm sorry," Raven said stroking Lady Majiks neck. She had freed Silverdrake -but at what cost?

"Hope and faith...I have both," whispered Lady Majik softly encouraging Raven.

And they were off. Sunbeam was galloping at full speed with Raven and Alfie holding on for dear life. Rat was in the backpack rattling up and down. He was holding the yellow potion, desperate to take a drop. He missed home. Raven smiled as the rain battered off her face, she was riding a unicorn. Despite the horrible ordeal she felt light as a feather, Majika truly was magical. With the mountain close Raven felt a fire burning in her bones. She had to succeed.

Night was falling and the relentless rain made it hard to focus. Sunbeam slowed down to a canter then a trot before walking. When her eyes focused, she stopped dead in her tracks. The tall mountain was a bundle of rocks shaped like a triangle. Circling at the bottom was a million goblins. Every goblin in Majika was at the very same mountain.

"OH NO!" cried Alfie. If he seen another goblin in a million moons it would have been too soon.

*Why are they here? They must be working with Darcy,* thought Raven angrily. How could one human be so stupid and selfish?

"I'll be bait," said Sunbeam. If there was one thing goblins wanted more than Raven it was unicorn's blood.

"There are so many," Raven said panicked. Sunbeam did not have the magical powers her mother had. Her magic had disappeared as soon as the crystal skull was taken.

"Dismount here and on my neigh find a gap and start climbing," ordered Sunbeam rearing. Her hoofs kicked in the air furiously. Then she charged at lightning speed. She galloped towards them with a              brave              heart..

# HOPE

Raven and Alfie were close to the top - their hands wet, cut and sore from climbing the rocks. The rain had softened and the moon was out; a big bright moon, lighting up the horror below. The evil mist was almost upon them. Sunbeam was furiously grunting, kicking, bucking and rearing far below their eyes. The never-ending rows of goblins were launching themselves at her. Attacking the royal from all angles. She was tiring. Her snow-white coat now blood stained.

Alfie wanted to cry. He wanted his mother. Fear ran through his body like a pack of wolves. He could not control his mind from thinking the worst. *Stone statue, munched by goblins or falling off this mountain!* They had been climbing for almost an hour. Rat was still in the backpack, curled into his little pillow shivering. The bag was now damp from all the rain. He would force Raven to drink the 'go home' potion if he had to.

"Darcy…" whispered Raven holding a hand in front of Alfie. They ducked in behind the rocks. Raven gave Alfie's hand a squeeze. She knew the water running down his cheeks was not the rain.

 Darcy was tall, dressed head to toe in black. Her brown hair tied back in a long plait. She opened up a box, as she peeled back the lid an explosion of pure white light came out. She held the skull in her hands. It was the size of a human head. The crystal looked jagged. The mouth was slightly open exposing glistening diamond teeth.

"Almost time. Final point," laughed Darcy loudly, holding the skull towards the sky. She stood at the peak of the mountain on an unsteady rock.

 The grey mist had reached Sunbeam now. The beautiful brave unicorn lay badly wounded, unable to run. The evil goblins fled for the mountain bouncing and leaping upwards quicker than humanly possible. Raven and Alfie could hear their cackling below. Alfie's body shook uncontrollably.

Rovi had explained that those who touch the skull cannot be turned to stone. They had to get to it before the goblins got to them. They had to move fast.

"Don't do it Darcy," Raven shouted climbing out from behind the rock. Raven's damp hair stuck to her face. Her waterproofs were oversized and torn from the climb.

"Get them!" screamed Darcy as the goblins got closer. She pointed her finger at Raven laughing. Darcy had promised to take the goblins back to earth to eat humans for breakfast, lunch, and dinner. Stupid goblins believed her.

"So much for the prophecy," she cackled.

"We are going to DIE!!!" screamed Alfie looking at the goblins shiny fangs heading their way.

But in the darkest of despair, there is always hope. All was not doomed. Cold gusts of air hit

Raven off her feet. Alfie screamed even louder as they were being circled by ghosts. Not just any ghosts, it was the ghosts from the Earth Walker graveyard. They began to chant, forming a protective barrier around Raven and Alfie.

"Thank you," whispered Raven as the goblins slowed down. If the animal ghosts hadn't come the goblins would have no doubt been ripping their flesh from their bodies by now.

A screech came from the sky. Fire streamed towards the goblins sending them tumbling backwards like dominos. The ghosts floated upwards and disappeared.

"Silverdrake!" cried Raven tearful. He was free and the Crystal Skull was in sight.

"Relax, Elf," Willow appeared from nowhere sprinkling some gold dust over Alfie. He instantly felt better. He didn't know if it was her magic or because the biggest, scariest fire breathing dragon was on their side. The goblins were fleeing like scared mice jumping into the mist willingly. Turning

65

to stone in midair.

"What, NOOOOOO!" wailed Darcy. Silverdrake flew towards her, his red eyes burning. The rock she was on started to wobble. She lost her balance. Raven threw herself forward to catch the crystal skull as it flew through the air. It landed safely in her hands.

Darcy was gone. She was falling from a great height, screaming. Silverdrake swooped down and caught Darcy's leather jacket by his teeth. She closed her eyes thinking one nip and she was a goner!   He flew her back to the peak of the mountain narrowly escaping the mist. Darcy dropped with a thud back on the rock.

"Sorry I took so long," roared the dragon! He had been waiting for the moon to fully charge him. Willow sat on her best friend's head, glowing like a torch. Raven and Alfie wasted no time climbing up his tail and onto his back. His scales stuck out slightly giving them something to hold onto.

Raven zipped the skull safely inside her oversized jacket and shouted to Rat it was almost home time.

She looked at Darcy; the mist would be with her in minutes.

"Bring Darcy," Raven said feeling merciful, she knew the goblins would kill her once the mist spell was broken.

Silverdrake took to the air, grabbing Darcy's leather jacket in his teeth once more. She dangled powerless kicking and screaming, unable to use her powers.

They had the Crystal Skull and the thief. But at what cost, thought Raven, with a tear trickling down her cheek as she seen wounded Sunbeam lying still as stone.

Silverdrake let out a screech that echoed throughout the land. Darcy's ears were ringing! The enormous fire breathing dragon was free… and it was thanks to a small girl with a kind brave heart.

# GREED

Raven placed the crystal skull on its rightful place in the pillar. It locked down, fitting perfectly like a jigsaw piece. A burst of light exploded, Raven ducked down closing her eyes. It was so bright. Rainbows appeared swooping and looping all around the grand Hall of Happiness, they dissolved the stone in the room before multiplying and whooshing out the windows and doors.

"Rainbows on a mission," chuckled a rather handsome tall elf stretching. He had been turned to stone with his hands in the air -very uncomfortable.

Darcy was weeping loudly in the courtyard. Willow was giving her a right ear bashing. The little fairy was super upset- not only because Darcy had nearly destroyed Majika. She was hurt by Darcy's lies. She thought they were friends. Lady Majik trotted over to them. She felt pity for tearful Darcy, now sobbing into a handkerchief by the dragon waterfall.

"I'm sorry your Majesty," Darcy stood up and bowed her head slightly. She hung her head in shame as multiple pairs of eyes stared at her angrily.

Lady Majik paused. The prophecy had come true – the gifted human that could speak to animals saved Majika and freed Silverdrake as a bonus. If Darcy had not committed such a terrible crime, Silverdrake would not be free. Rovi told the Royals of Darcy's first trip to Majika when she was only ten. She hated her teleporting gift; she had woken up in coal bunkers, and hay stacks, even found herself in her PJ's in a school playground once. Rovi had asked Willow to guide her to Lina - the very best fae witch in Pinerock Valley to learn to control her powers.

"Off with her head!" chanted the growing crowd.

"Leave her for the goblins!" screamed some angry elf's.

Willow panicked. She did not want that punishment for Darcy.

The palace gates flew open and in hobbled Sunbeam with a limp. By her side stood a mysterious lady wrapped in a purple velvet hooded cloak. Raven ran - jumping over pots of flowers. She lunged herself at Sunbeam, cuddling into her neck.

"You're alive!" Raven cried hugging the Royal tightly.

"Will take more than a million goblins to bring me down," she joked winking at Alfie. Alfie was now crying with happiness. He loved happy endings.

The lady pulled down her hood. Her dark eyes sparkled. She gave Raven a gentle pat on the head.

"Greeting royals," her voice was loud and firm. She sounded like a head teacher.

"Firstly, Professor Chutney apologises for his

absence. He is still recovering from being a stone statue." she pointed a long finger at Darcy.

"Lina how wonderful! We were just talking about you." Lady Majik welcomed her.

"Yes, well. Pinerock valley is a trek away. And the cherry pie is better on my side of the world," said Lina matter of fact.

"True," agreed Alfie. He had once walked for fourteen moons for a piece of Pinerock's pie.

Lina looked at Darcy. With a pointed finger she lifted her off the ground and pulled her flying through the air towards her. Darcy looked at Lina for several seconds then itched her pointy nose. Darcy dropped in front of her.

"Sorry. My friends made fun of me because I didn't have...I just wanted the best phone and computer and..." cried Darcy.

"Ohh shhhh Darcy. Pull yourself together," Lina snapped.

"I spent many moons on earth. Darcy has fallen victim to the disease so many humans have. It's

71

called GREED!" she snapped at Darcy again.

"A good girl like you should know better. If your friends don't like you for who you are then they are not worth being your friends." Lina spoke softer and helped Darcy to her feet.

"All's well that ends well," Lady Majik agreed. The sun was rising, the sky bursting with a mash of pink, red and yellows.

"The tremble of the mist has left quite a mess in Professor Chutney's lab. Fairy dust is everywhere. He is most displeased. Miss Darcy will be cleaning like Cinderella before she returns home," Lina looked at Lady Majik who nodded in agreement. Cleaning with Professor Chutney was a suitable punishment. He was a grumpy old professor with a long white dirty beard and really bad breath.

Darcy sighed. Better than being eaten by goblins.

"I'll be seeing you at the masquerade magical ball next. Thank you for our invite." said Lina turning around with Darcy's hand in hers.

Willow circled around Darcy's her head like a

torpedo. A visit to Pinerock valley was long overdue.

"This time you can ride up front." she nudged Darcy playfully on the cheek. Silverdrake was waiting on the grass outside the palace gates.

Silverdrake took to the sky with Lina, Darcy and Willow. Lina clicked her fingers. An almighty BANG exploded very high in the sky. The most magical fireworks display exploded into a puff of colours in the shape of a skull.

"That is for you, brave Raven," said Lady Majik.

# GOODBYES

"Breakfast banquet before Raven and Rat go home!" A tall elf announced. Officially inviting everyone to a morning party. Everyone cheered. White sparkles danced from her the queen's horn. The Great Hall of Happiness now looked fit for a wedding. Jolly music filled the room. Bouquets of yellow roses, danced joyfully in mid-air. The cutlery was dancing on top of the crinkle free white table cloths. Pretty white and lemon china plates were piled high with delicious food. Alfie and Rats faces lit up with joy. Rat nearly had a mouse attack when he seen a bowl of peanut butter. All the diamonds in the world couldn't make him smile more.

Lady Majik looked at Raven. This would not do! Damp knotted hair ripped jackets and trousers. Cut and bruised hands! Her horn beamed again, this time the fashion fairies danced around Raven covering her in a blue cloud. Alfie and Rat were being circled also. Little measuring tapes danced around them.

Alfie looked at Raven. His jaw wide open. She was beautiful. Her hair smooth and sitting perfectly down by her waist, she was in a black and red ball gown, encrusted with diamonds around the hem. Very goth princess! The cuts and bruises had gone and a white marble dragon pendant was hanging around her neck.

"Thank you, Lady Majik," gushed Raven clasping the pendant. She loved it. Her cheeks burned pink as everyone started to compliment her appearance. Alfie was rather handsome too in a red velvet suit. Rat found it all very funny until a matching jacket appeared on him.

"Noooo!" screamed Rat. He felt hideous.

The Great Hall of Happiness was bursting with laughter. Everyone was tucking into a breakfast buffet fit for a queen.

Alfie got presented with a warrior's badge - which he accepted in tears. A small, plump elf arrived towards the end of the party. She tugged his ear before kissing him on the cheek. His mother was panicked and relieved to see her son, alive. She was beaming with pride and could not wait to show off his badge at Elfinstone Valley.

Raven wasn't one for goodbyes. She had had the best adventure ever and made some of the weirdest, coolest, most unlikely friends along the way. To say goodbye brought a lump to her throat. She did not know when or if she would see them again. Lady Majik neighed, grateful that the prophecy had come true. She watched Raven and Rat drink the bitter sweet 'go home' potion with joy in her heart. Majika was save for another moon and even safer now Silverdrake was free.

"Oh, and for the record, Rat is braver than me," chuckled Alfie through streaming eyes.

"I will miss you all," smiled Raven feeling sleepy.

# NEW SCHOOL

Raven begged her mum not to kiss her goodbye at the school gates. But she did anyway. *First embarrassment of the day,* thought Raven, hoping no one had noticed. Primrose Primary was bigger than her last school. It was a fancy building, all cream and glass. The uniform was hideous. Rat had laughed himself to the toilet when he seen Raven in the dark red pleated skirt and matching woolly jumper. She reminded Rat of a huge tomato!

The bell rang loudly. Children darted with their matching uniforms in all directions. Raven headed to the school office.  A small lady with curly white hair and a face full of makeup ushered Raven to her new classroom. Raven took a deep breath. This was more nerve racking than being chased by goblins.

The office lady opened the door. Raven stood inside staring at over twenty new faces. She clasped the dragon pendant around her neck.

"Take a seat your new teacher will be here in a few minutes," and the lady was gone. Raven felt like an antelope dropped into a pack of lions. Everyone stopped chattering and stared at her. Raven took a big breath. If she could survive falling through candy floss clouds, sleeping in a tree, a goblin attack and riding a fire breathing dragon plus saving an entire world she'd manage the first day at a new school.

"Hello," Raven said quietly scanning the room for a seat. There was an empty table at the very back next a red-haired girl.

"You don't want to sit next to IT," laughed a tall boy with blonde spiky hair.

The girl blushed and dropped her head.

"She's weird," laughed a pretty blonde girl. Other girls laughed along with her.

"Weird is good, I like weird," Raven said smiling. She walked past their table with her head held high. She had saved Majika, been chased by goblins and rode a fire breathing dragon. She knew all about weird and she had begun to like it.

"Hey, my name is Raven," Raven noticed her hands had thin cream gloves on.

"April, my name is April," the girl said nervously, looking at the plant pots lined up along the window. There were tiny little bulbs poking through.

"It's really nice to meet you," smiled Raven. The girl relaxed. Raven heard chatter from behind. She turned to see a small fat ginger hamster in a cage complaining about the lack of honey seeds in his bowl.

"Oh, that's Donny, the classroom hamster," giggled April. She liked the grumpy hamster.

Raven couldn't concentrate - Donny's complaining was beginning to drive her insane.

"Hey Donny, please stop complaining and I'll bring

you more honey nut seed sticks than you can eat tomorrow." Raven whispered quietly at the cage. The hamster paused in shock. He clasped his paws together. It was a miracle; all his hamster prayers had been answered.

April looked at Raven. "Animal whisperer," guessed April excitedly. "My sister told me we weren't the only gifted humans." April pulled off her gloves and held her hands up facing one of the plant pots. Green thorn stalks pushed up through the soil until they were fully grown. A yellow rose burst open as the door knocked loudly. April quickly pulled on her gloves.

"So cool! What can your sister do?" Raven asked impressed. Finally, she had a friend that believed her.

"Darcy can teleport," April said thinking about her annoying big sister. She was forever playing pranks on her.

Raven's jaw hung open. April was Darcy's little sister. Raven was happy the elfin warriors hadn't fed her to the goblins. That would have been a little awkward.

Before she could ask the million questions running through her mind the teacher coughed loudly.

"Greetings all," said the lady loudly commanding attention.

The class went silent staring at their odd new teacher in a long hooded black cloak - her hair was silvery grey and touched her waist. Her skin was old and wrinkly but her eyes looked young and sparkled blue. The pendant hanging around her neck was a snow-white bird.

"You can call me Ms Esmeralda." she winked at Raven.

Raven smiled. She felt happy. This school year was going to be very different.

Raven had come to learn that different was not always weird. Different was being an individual, being yourself. She knew now that being different could be good - it could be amazing.

Raven couldn't wait to get home and tell Rat

about her first day at school.   Maybe not about Donny though – he'd get hamster envy...

*Magic is believing in yourself,*
*Do that,*
*And you can do anything!*

Printed in Great Britain
by Amazon